DAMEON YOUNG

to follow your Dreams
everything needs a STRONG

FOUNDATION

FOUNDATION

Dameon Young

Not Just Alphabets Publishing and its affiliates recognize the importance of preserving what has been written. To print the books, we publish on acid-free paper and we will continue to produce excellence.

THE LIBRARY OF CONGRESS HAS CATALOGED THIS MANUSCRIPT EDITION AS FOLLOWS:

Copyright © Dameon Young 2019

ISBN: 978-1-7338810-0-5

LCCN:

Editor/Layout Cover Design

Printed in the United States of America

To everyone who Dreams of someday writing a Book…

you can do it, keep writing.

- dameon young -

Acknowledgements

First and foremost all credit to my Lord and Savior for thinking enough of me to give me this extraordinary talent. Secondly, to my first cousin Shay "Hogg" Kinney. The only person to pick me up when I was at my lowest, telling me with undeniable confidence it wasn't over for me. He believed in me when I didn't. For that, I owe you everything little brother. My mother for keeping her foot on my neck and refusing to let me rest. Forcing me to keep going and giving me the impression that nothing I did was good enough. You made me bring my best, no matter the occasion, love you for that Ma... you created a monster. My Big Mama and Big Daddy for showing me consistency and commitment works. My Aunt Jackie, Aunt San, Uncle Gary, Uncle Jerome. My cousins Brandon Madden, Sam Kinney, Niecy Kinney, and Alfonzo Madden. Cartez Taylor for being there when I needed to vent. My brother from another mother, Matthew Coleman. Years ago you told me I had a gift, it didn't register back then, but I'm tuned in now baby boy. A. J. Houston for being that positive role model I was missing and always answering my calls and questions. You a real one my brother, and to all my siblings, love y'all. You all had a major impact on my life. To my precious kids, daddy love y'all. When I tell y'all anything is possible, I mean that. The sky is the limit for us, so let's abuse it! All the doubters, stay on your job, y'all make every victory a little more sweeter.

CHAPTER 1

There once was a man who went by the name of Grateful. He had the best attitude you could find, but the worst luck imaginable. He lived in a rundown shed in the back of an abandoned house. He was that guy who would offer you the shirt off his back, but no one ever accepted because it had an odor that you could smell a few feet away. Anyhow, Grateful met a very successful and wealthy businessman at one of the corner store's he'd often go to and clean to keep some food in his stomach. He'd seen the man on many occasions and spoken to him each time. It was always a simple "Hi" and "Bye," but nothing special. This day was different. The man walked over to him and asked him, "How does a man clean a store as impeccable as you do for crumbs, because I am almost certain they don't pay you what you deserve. I come in this store every morning on my way to work and it smells horrible, but on my way home when I stop by it looks and smells like a totally different store?"

"Well, it's easy. No matter if you're a big shot from Wallstreet or a person who clean these (hole in the wall) businesses for little of nothing, you have to give it your all." "Love the positivity and passion. Here's twenty bucks, grab you something to eat tonight on me. Can you meet me here in the morning at 6 a.m., There is a job I need done that will put some real money in your pocket." "Thank you, kind sir, and yes, I can and will meet you here in the morning," responds Grateful. "Alright partner sounds good. I guess I'll see you in a.m." "O.k., see you in the morning. What is your name?" asks Grateful. "Call me Lucky. Everybody calls me Lucky." "Alright

Lucky. Thank you for the opportunity," says Grateful graciously. "Don't thank me yet, just be here on time and be ready to work." "Most definitely," responds Grateful before Lucky leaves.

The next morning Grateful arrives at the store around 5:50 a.m. A few minutes later Chin, the guy who owned the corner store pulls up. "Good morning Mr. Chin," says Grateful. "Good morning Grateful. I won't have anything for you to do until later, sorry," Chin says in his deep Korean accent. "Thank you for the consideration, but that's not why I'm here." "Oh, ok. Is everything alright?" asks Chin. "Everything is wonderful. Just waiting on a friend," answers Grateful. "Ok. Don't get into any trouble. Will you be back later?" "I don't know, but if so I will come by and see if you need my help". "Ok, see you soon," responds Chin as he unlocks the doors to the store and goes in. A few moments after Chin goes in, a white Ford F -150 pulls into the parking lot and pulls over to were Grateful was waiting. "You ready?" asks Lucky from the driver side of the truck. "Yes, I am," says Grateful as he throws his bag on the back of the truck and hops in.

After a short ride across town, the two of them pull into a large field with a two-story house on the Northwest side of the field with a few large oak trees scattered throughout the property. Lucky pulls his truck under one of the large trees closest to the house. "Alright Grateful, you see that house right there?," "Of course I do,, responds Grateful. "Well, my fiancé, Leslie and I are expecting our first child, and this is the home that we would like to bring her home to, but

11

there's one small problem. It's an old house and there's a few problems with the foundation. It needs to be reconstructed, you know, strengthened a little bit. That's what I need your help with. I heard you were a pretty decent labor man and I am willing to pay you good for your services." "If that's all you need I can help you with that," responds Grateful. "That's what I was hoping to hear. There's only one catch. I can't commute you here every day and this job will take a few days. So, my idea is to leave you here for three days and come back on the third day, pick you up and pay you, then drop you back off wherever you need to go. There's a spare bedroom in the very back of the house with a radio and mattress. Are you comfortable with that?" "Just in case you didn't notice, I'm not in a situation to turn down any work. So, to answer your question, yes, I will be much obliged. What am I going to do about food though," asked Grateful? "Don't worry about that. I packed a cooler with enough food and drinks to last you a week. Whatever you don't eat while out here you can take with you," responded Lucky. "That's very thoughtful of you Mr. Lucky. I have no problems with those stipulations." "Sounds good. Let's get this truck unpacked so you can get to work then." "Let's do it," says Grateful, as he gets out of the truck, lets the tailgate down and starts to unload the supplies.

"Ok, I brought cement, two-by-fours, plywood, a drill, drill bits, screws, a hammer, nails, and some cement blocks. This should be more than enough supplies for you to get the job done. Whatever you don't use leave in a pile and we will load it back up when I pick you up." Grateful continues to unload the supplies as Lucky walks over to the house. He puts everything into some organized piles. The cement and cement blocks into a pile, the hammer, nails, drill, drill bits, and screws into a pile, and the two-by-fours and plywood into a pile. By the time he's done, Lucky is walking back towards him from the house. "I unlocked the door for you. You can find towels, tissue and other toiletries in the restroom and paper plates, paper cups, and plasticware in the bedroom. There is running water so feel free to shower whenever you need to. Oh, I almost forgot about the cooler. Its heavy so we both will have to carry it into the bedroom. Grab a hold of it so I can show you to your room," says Lucky as he jumps onto the bed of the truck and drags the cooler to the tailgate.

After carrying the cooler to the backroom, Lucky shows Grateful the restroom, and leads him into the kitchen. Here is the table so you can sit in comfort to eat or just sit to rest after a long day's work. "Alright Grateful, I think I've hung around long enough. Ima get to work and allow you to do the same," says Lucky, as the two of them walk back out to the truck. "Ok, Grateful. I am going to trust you with my home, please don't disappoint or disrespect me." "You have nothing to worry about. I will treat it with the utmost respect while you're gone sir." "I trust you will. I wouldn't have brought you out here if I felt otherwise. I just wanted to hear you say that for a little reassurance. With that being said, I am going to leave you here and I will return in three days". "Alright boss, drive safe." As Lucky drives off, Grateful begins to get all of his tools and supplies in order.

CHAPTER 2

After three days of work, Lucky arrives, just as he said. It was 5:30 in the morning, still dark outside. He saw Grateful sitting out front on the stairs of the house. As Lucky parks the truck, Grateful walks over towards him. "Good morning," says Lucky. "Good morning," answers Grateful. "So, how'd it turns out?" asked Lucky as he looked at the foundation of the house. "Why don't you tell me?" asked Grateful as he walked toward the southeast corner of the lot. "Where are you going?" asked Lucky. "To show you your new foundation."

"No, no, no! There has been a terrible misunderstanding!" screams Lucky as he runs and cuts Grateful off. "I brought you out here to restore the foundation of my house, not for you to do some kind of workshop experiment." Lucky yells as his face turns as red as the cigarette box in his shirt pocket. As Lucky stomps towards the southeastern corner of the lot, it is still dark outside, so Lucky cannot see what Grateful constructed through the darkness, at the time, he really didn't care.

"You have wasted all of the materials I brought out here, not to mention both of our times. Now I understand why you're in the situation you're in. You CAN NOT follow simple instr…" and at that very moment, while he was yelling, the eastern sun began to rise over the horizon and he gotta peek at what Grateful built. It was beautiful. A huge cross held up by a perfectly landscaped bed of cement, with colorful roses, bonnets, sunflowers and a natural earth colored mulch all created in a flowerbed around the cement and cement blocks. The more the sun peeked over the background, the more everything was illuminated and the more Lucky fell in love with his new foundation. After about three minutes of silence, Lucky walks over to Grateful, now calmer than ever and tells him. "I get it... I get it. I understand. Without this foundation (he points to the cross), that foundation (he points to the house) will never last or be strong enough to raise a family the correct way."

"I'm glad you can finally see things the way they are meant to be seen," says Grateful. "I am sorry for losing my temper Grateful," says an apologetic Lucky. "It's fine brother, I could have crawled under the house and built a brand-new structure underneath there out of cement and stone, but without the Lord's foundation, this home or no home would be truly fit to raise a family in." "Thank you Grateful. You have really opened my eyes. Shame on me for being so blind that I could not truly see what was in front of me. I have been so busy lately, I have not thought of giving the Lord His proper praise. How has a man with as much thought and wisdom as you end up poor? I just don't understand."

"Well Lucky, I am not poor. I may not have the monetary and visible riches as you, but I do have something of much more value. It's called favor. The Good Lord never allows me to go hungry or weary. He supplies all of my needs and keeps me safe and strong enough to productively work and spread love to those who need it." "Very well said Grateful. I guess the only thing left to do is to go to the bank and get you some money," says Lucky. "Sounds good to me. Hop in the truck and let's get outta here. And while we are riding, we can discuss when you're going to come back and put some support under my house," says Lucky, rephrasing his request.

CHAPTER 3

Lucky goes to the bank and withdraws five thousand bucks and hands it to Grateful. "I cannot thank you enough for enlightening me this morning. What you did for my family was priceless." "I am doing nothing, but GOD'S will. No more no less," says Grateful. Lucky pulls his truck under a shade tree near the exit of the bank. "I'm a man of my word Grateful. I told you I would pay you good if you gave me a foundation and you did that, so I must stand on my end of the bargain and pay you," he says as he counts out fifty-one hundred-dollar bills.

"Thank you for trusting me enough to give me the opportunity," says Grateful as he gets the money that Lucky placed on the armrest. "There's five grand. I think that should be more than enough to get a wise man like yourself off these streets and into a descent apartment and maybe even some transportation," says Lucky. "I've always been more of a sharer, but if it is the Lord's will it shall be done," says Grateful. "Very well spoken my new-found friend. Very well spoken," says Lucky as he pulls out of the parking lot. Grateful asks Lucky to drop him at some nearby hotel rooms instead of at the corner store so he could get a decent night's rest. "Well, I don't see why not, it's just right around the corner. Plus, the way I look at it a comfortable bed and a stomach full will make a man feel like a man," responds Lucky.

As they pull into the hotel parking lot Grateful tells Lucky to drop him off at the office, so he could go ahead and check in. "Alright, here you go buddy, front door service," says Lucky as he parks directly in front of the office building. "Here's my phone number, gimme a call early next week. I'd like to keep in contact with you," says Lucky. "Sounds good. Write your information down on a piece of paper for me and we'll take it from there," responds Grateful. "Alright buddy. You take care of yourself and stay wise, it'll pay off enormously," says Lucky as he hands him the folded piece of paper with his phone number on it. "Thank you for the opportunity once again Lucky. You have truly been a blessing," says Grateful as he grabs his bags out of the truck. "No worries. I think the appreciation is mutual," says Lucky. "Indeed," says Grateful as he extends his hand to shake Lucky's hand. "See you around buddy," says Lucky before pulling out of the hotel parking lot.

3 Years Later…

Lucky sits at the table of a high-end restaurant on the thirteenth floor of one of the tallest buildings in the city awaiting the arrival of his guest. As he sits there, he sees a bird, which he assumes is a mama bird, land on the window sill directly in front of his table with a worm in its beak. The bird carries the worm over to a nest where three baby birds await and allows them to eat while it rests. The mama bird doesn't even attempt to eat. As it carefully watches it's little one's eat, afterwards it settles for what the baby birds didn't eat, a typical mother's actions.

After about twenty minutes of waiting, Grateful arrives with a suitcase in his hands. Over the past three years, Grateful and Lucky became really close. They were business partners, best friends, and Grateful was the God father to Lucky's son. Lucky even loaned Grateful the funds to open his own Landscaping service. Grateful paid him back with interest, in half of the time they agreed upon. That made Lucky trust him even more.

"Good morning," says Grateful, as he sits down at the table and places the suitcase on the floor. "What you got there?" asks Lucky. "A very attractive business proposition for the both of us, if you're interested," responds Grateful confidently. "Shoot your shot," says Lucky. "Okay," says Grateful as he grabs the suitcase from the floor, opens it and sat it on the table. "These are the blueprints to a shelter I drew up." Grateful takes out the papers and slides them across the table to Lucky. "But this isn't going to be a regular shelter. This shelter is going to be ran by us but operated by the homeless. The idea is to make as many of the less fortunate as possible a self-sufficient and productive members of society."

"We will place twenty to thirty of them in a home and let them operate it in shifts. Each shift has a receptionist, cooks, custodial workers, outside workers, and maintenance workers. Everyone else will have jobs off the property. I'm talking bringing people in that will thoroughly train these guys for success. We can train them on HVAC, electrical, construction, painting, landscaping, healthcare, business management, and simple warehouse work like forklift driv-

ers, order pullers, loaders, unloaders, etc. If we allow them to im-
prove their work skills by training them, we can change a lot of lives.
Each of them will have to put fifteen percent of their monthly in-
come towards the home which will teach and/or re-teach them re-
sponsibility," says Grateful as he waits on Lucky's response. "What
you are proposing is a shelter meets temp service kind of idea?," responds Lucky. "Exactly, but I would like to look at it as a shelter
meets temp service meets re-entry into productivity program."

"If we cross our T's and dot all of our I's, we can get the
state to fund this program one hundred percent, and everyone's happy. Less vagrants, more jobs and a cleaner city. No one loses," says
Grateful. "That sounds great, we are going to have to get a lot of
powerful signatures just to get the ball rolling," says Lucky. "Let's get
it started then. I'm ready to proceed," responds Grateful. "I know
you are, but Grateful, something like this takes time. Your idea
sounds perfect to me but there are people that get paid to do nothing but listen to great ideas like yours and pick them apart. They will
try to find holes in them only to ruin their dreams. Let's take our
time, go over this slowly and carefully. Then we can present it to the
powers that be. Trust me, this can be a colossal game changer we
both can retire from. An idea like this must be planned beyond per-
fection before we can consider a start date, nonetheless a completion
date."

CHAPTER 4

After about five to six months of doing nothing but running their business by day and trying to find an investor by night, both men began to get very frustrated and lose faith in humanity. Most of the people they talked to wouldn't give them time to explain after they found out the type of people, they were going to let run the facility. They all thought it would be a waste of money. They believed the place would stay trashed or the tenants would steal everything of value at first opportunity. That is, until Grateful met a southern gentleman from Arkansas named Gary Alexander. Mr. Alexander started with a trucking company, hauling grain and feed. Over time he bought it from the owner and turned it into a conglomerate. Mr. Alexander saw the same silver lining in their vision that they did. A small sacrifice towards bettering humanity.

Grateful met with him for two days straight before Lucky was introduced to him. He wanted to be sure before moving on. Mr. Alexander never seemed reluctant, hesitant, or bothered by anything he heard. He gave the impression he was into second or even third chances. That's when he was as sure as he had ever been. This was the link they had been missing. Now it was time to take it a step further and introduce him to Lucky.

The three of them met at a high-end steak house. The conversation lasted for hours over steaks, baked potatoes, and an eighty -five-year-old bottle of Chardonnay. The first hour they didn't even discuss business, they talked about early childhood experiences, religion, family, sports, literature, beliefs and cars. They spoke on the mistakes made that got them where they are today. Not one of them was reserved or shy about revealing any of the truths from their past. They understood life was a process of mistakes, learning, and accepting the person they are today. They talked of how making thoughtful decisions will make them better and more efficient than the person they were in the past. So far, the night has exceeded expectations on a personal and a business level, all of them agreed on that. As a matter of fact, there were only a few things they disagreed on the entire night. They all wanted to better humanity and change lives, all in the name of Faith.

As the three gentlemen sat around the table laughing, talking and preparing for what lies ahead, whether good, bad, expected, or unexpected. Grateful grabs his suitcase off the floor and pulls out his rough draft blueprint of the building and grounds of the property. He had a list of estimated monthly expenses, including payroll, insurance and upkeep of the facility inside and out. "This is all of the necessary paperwork we need to move forward. All of these numbers were generated from their proper jurisdictions. So, everything you see, will be as accurate as one's research can allow. Some months we may go over, some months we may go under, but we will always land somewhere near the vicinity of these numbers," says Grateful. "You weren't kidding when you said you like your businesses in order, jeesh," said Mr. Alexander, as he reached in his blazer for his glasses to assist him with looking over the paperwork. "Do you have anything you would like to add before we close this agreement?" he asked Lucky. "No, I don't. My business partner is as thorough as they come. Any and everything of relevance, significance, or importance to this project, I trust is in that stack of papers," says Lucky as he sips his Latte and looks over his glasses at the paperwork. "Well, I guess there's nothing else to do but sign some papers and write a check," says Mr. Alexander as he pulls out his checkbook.

While Mr. Alexander was looking over the paperwork, Grateful decided to run to his truck and grab the color of pen needed to make the signatures on the paperwork valid. He exited the restaurant, reached in his pocket for the keys and proceeded to cross the street to his truck. Then out of nowhere, he was hit by a speeding car with its lights off. He was hit so hard, he was knocked twelve feet into the air before landing on the cold pavement. He was knocked unconscious and lay on the ground with several broken bones all alone, with help nowhere in sight. He lay on the concrete partially broken and bleeding very badly for about fifteen minutes, before he was found by a couple leaving the restaurant. When they first saw him, they thought he was just another drunk who had more than he could handle, until they got close enough to see all the blood. The woman let out a blood curdling scream. It was loud enough to catch the attention of an off-duty police officer, walking on the opposite side of the street. "Ma'am, what's the problem," asked the officer as he approached her? "THIS MAN NEEDS MEDICAL ASSISTANCE RIGHT NOW!!!" she screamed. The officer reached in his pocket for his phone as he ran across the street. "Oh my God," said the officer, as he shined his flashlight on Grateful. "Hold on buddy," says the officer as he leans over him and radios for the ambulance. At the same time Lucky was exiting the restaurant to see what was taking Grateful so long. He steps out and notices a small crowd forming a few feet from Grateful's truck. He yells his name and runs towards the crowd. "What happened?" he asked, while pushing people out of the way to get to his friend. "OH GOD, NO!" says Lucky franticly. The only thing recognizable to Lucky was Grateful bloody clothes. He was so swollen he looked like a totally different person. "MOVE," screams Lucky towards the off-duty officer. "GET OFF OF HIM," he continues, pushing the officer again. This time, pushing him to the ground. "Sir, I am a police officer trying to help. If you want your friend to get some help, you need to calm down and let me help him," says the officer as he gets off the ground. "Did you do this to him?" asked Lucky, as he got more and more aggressive with the cop. "Of course not, I'm trying to help dude!" says the officer as he's being slung around like a doll. "Sir, please relax. We found him like this. Acting like this is not going to help your friend at all," says the woman who found Grateful, as she tries to calm Lucky down. By this time the ambulance arrived and begin attending to Grateful, but it was looking very bad.

CHAPTER 5

Lucky paced in circles in the hospitals waiting room, while Mr. Alexander sat quietly in the corner staring at the ceiling. Suddenly, the surgeon appears from around a sharp corner looking fatigued in a pair of sky-blue scrubs. He walks straight over to Lucky, never breaking eye contact as if he already knew who he was and says, "I'm Doctor Jerome Madden, your friend Grateful suffered a lot of swelling, some internal bleeding, multiple lacerations, and a few broken bones. The first procedure was a success. We were able to stop the bleeding and get him stitched up. He suffered a broken clavicle and two broken fibula, which we were able to fuse back together and place a strong cast around, but unfortunately; due to all of his injuries we had to induce him into a coma. That's not as bad as it sounds, because we were able keep his blood pressure constant. We placed him in a coma to give his body time for the swelling to go down. This will help us get a clearer picture of any possible organ damage."
'

"How long will he be in a coma?" asks Lucky. "I apologize but I can't answer that question at the moment. It depends on how his body reacts to the procedure and his willpower to keep living," responds Doctor Madden. "Look Doc, is there anything you can do? I need him awake. We were on the verge of doing something very special and beneficial that would affect a lot of people," says Lucky. "You may need him awake, but he needs to be asleep for his own sake. I'm sure whatever it was you all were on the verge of, can be postponed for a short time. Trust me, we are doing everything we can to get him up and running at one hundred percent."

"With the severity of his injuries, one wrong move can be very painful and at worst, detrimental. Especially if he slips or falls, he can be in big trouble. So, could you please be patient and understanding of our very carefully thought out procedure's sir," says Dr. Madden, then calmly walks off. Lucky is in a state of pure disbelief; his eyes are still fixated in the exact same spot as they were while he was talking to the Doctor. He was staring into nothingness.

While Lucky is still in a daze, Mr. Alexander walks over to him and calmly says, "My deepest sympathy goes out to you Lucky, it tru…" he is abruptly cut off by Lucky, "sympathy won't wake up my buddy now will it?" He says as he storms off.

CHAPTER 6

Three days later, the driver of the car that struck Grateful is apprehended and charged with four offenses. 1. vehicular assault, 2. leaving the scene of an accident, 3. failing to stop and render aid, and 4. a D.U.I. Lucky is contacted and updated with everything that is happening with the case. He attends every court date and does everything in his power to make sure this man pays for what he did to his friend. He attends the arraignment, bond hearing, and trial to show support for his comrade.

When the trial date finally arrives, he is there sitting front row. As he sits patiently waiting for the proceedings to begin, he feels a tap on the shoulder, it's Mr. Alexander. Lucky is surprised to see him. He gets up, turns, gives him a hug and thanks him for coming. "I really appreciate you for showing face buddy, it really means a lot to me. I know it means more to Grateful," he says as they shake hands. "I wouldn't have missed it for the world, what about you, how are you holding?" asked Mr. Alexander. "I've had better days," responds Lucky. "I believe you," says Mr. Alexander. "Because today, you look terrible. Have you been drinking," asked Mr. Alexander? "Are you here for support or are you here to be judgmental?" asked Lucky. "My good friend, I didn't mean that in a negative way but seeing you like this has completely caught me off guard." "Look, different people handle pressure differently, but the irony in that is pressure comes in two different forms. It can either put so much on you it will turn you into a diamond, or it's grasp will hold onto you, then squeeze you until you burst into an unrecognizable shell of your old self. I ask that you come into this courtroom with nothing but good energies, positive vibes, and an aura of love and support. You got me? This ain't the time for that," says Lucky as he fixes Mr. Alexander's collar and walks over to finds another seat.

At exactly nine o'clock, the judge nonchalantly walks out of a pair of red oak doors as the bailiff yells out, "All rise, as the Honorable Simpson Lamar resides." After Judge Lamar sits in his finely polished leather and red oak chair, the bailiff continues, "You all may now be seated." Everyone sits and the clerk stands to read the docket, case number, name of the plaintiff, and name of the defendant. While doing so the bailiff brings out a scruffy and underweight Caucasian male in an oversized orange jumpsuit. The judge reads him his charges then ask's him for a plea. "Your Honor, my client pleads not guilty, due to the combination of improper and misdiagnosed eye exams on top of fatigue. My client is not at fault here. We feel the deepest sympathy for the victim. If anyone should be at fault, it should be the inexperienced optometrist that disabled my client from a clear view of sight."

"Here are a few of the optometrists displeased patience statements and ratings this past year. May I add these are during his first year of business," says Mr. Jones, Mr. McElroy's lawyer as he places a stack of papers onto the judge's desk. The judge scans over them and says, "Due to the evidence at hand, I don't think we need to hear from the defense. Mr. McElroy doesn't have a criminal record nor any prior intoxication charges. I recommend the defendant be released with time served and placed on a stiff probation that requires him to check in three times a week, once over the phone, two times a week you must show up and give a physical urine sample."

"I order you get a breath analyzer installed in your vehicle within thirty days of today's date, at your expense. I also order you to pay court cost and restitution in full by the end of a six-month period starting today. You must attend and complete our substance abuse program. You must be available for home visits by your probation officer at any given time or date. Your probation officer must give you a courtesy call within two hours of the meeting time, you must show up and comply. If the defendant agrees, I dismiss all said charges except said charge of D.U.I., that is if your clients agrees to sign a plea of guilty to the D.U.I. charge."

"Does your client agree to these terms," the judge asks? Mr. McElroy looks at his attorney and nods. "Is there anything you would like to add Mr. McElroy," asks the judge. "No there is not judge. You've been more than fair," says McElroy as he smiles with an expression that says, "I just beat the system." The judge looks to the plaintiff, the woman Lucky hired to represent Grateful's case and says, "Mrs. Williams, is there anything you would like to add?" "As a matter of fact, there is," says Mrs. Williams. "The defendant's blood and alcohol level were three times the legal limit. Also, he was speeding down a congested street without using his head lights. That at least warrants a guilty verdict of reckless endangerment." "You are absolutely right counselor. That is if the defendant would have been prescribed the proper strength of eye glasses," says the judge. "But you honor…" she begins, but is rudely cut off by the judge. "Court is now adjourned," says the Judge before slamming his gavel.

CHAPTER 7

That same night, Lucky found himself sitting in the same poolhall he, Grateful, and Mr. Alexander sat in on the night of that terrible accident. He sat at a table by himself secluded in a corner. He ordered the double cheese, double meat house special with garlic onion fries. This was his favorite meal on the menu. Tonight he only took one bite of the burger, ate only a handful of fries, then pushed it to the side. Truly, he was not there for the house special, he had other plans. After leaving the courthouse and hearing the verdict he felt was unjust, he decided he was going to drink his life away.

He finally felt a sure sense of purpose in life, driven by nothing but positive energies and genuine love for mankind and in the blink of an eye, the opportunity faded away. Sure, he would have only been 1/3 owner, but the entirety of the idea came from Grateful and he (Grateful) refused to take a higher cut than his business partners. He wanted them to have as much credit as he did. That alone made Lucky feel happy enough to just be a part of it. Not because he was breaking even with his two business partners, but because he felt he finally found Loyalty outside of his home.

Unlike all of his other business ventures, this one would benefit others much more than it would benefit him. He had no doubt it would be a success, because for some reason, every task

Grateful attempted has been a success. He could not understand how so much talent was overlooked for so long and when it came time to be exposed, it ended as quickly as it began.

Lucky came from a wealthy family who owned plenty of businesses and stocks, they never worked hard a day in their life. He was trained at an early age to be a cutthroat businessman that could care less about the next man's feelings, opinions, or well-being. Before he met Grateful, his objective was to "provide plenty for self and let the rest get the scraps." So sad but true.

He felt so many emotions that day. He felt discouraged knowing he was a signature away from being a part of creating a legacy that would've lived years beyond him. He felt selfish for not spending more time at the hospital. His Faith felt betrayed by GOD because for all these years of doing wrong, he finally gave in and gave his life to The Lord and this happened. He wanted better for his life, new wife, and kid. He would get on his knees daily and pray for change and a renewal of Faith. That's when he felt Grateful was placed in his path, his angel in the most unexpected form ever imagined. A homeless vagrant sweeping, mopping, and taking out the trash of convenience store. He was working only to buy something to eat. Grateful was a man he passed on the streets almost every day for years. The type of person his elders taught him to avoid Only to discover he was the most talented, patient, honest, and faithful man he'd ever known. It is hard to believe when all of the stars align, YOU snatch him from me, where's the faith and loyalty in that? He thinks to himself. Oh well, he continues to think. That just goes to show, believing and religion is not all it's cracked up to be. He shakes his head in disbelief. He then calls the waitress over, "Bring me two double shots of the strongest whiskey you can find back there. While you at it bring me a pitcher of the coldest beer you can make, keep 'em coming," he tells the waitress. "Coming right out," she says as she walks towards the back.

CHAPTER 8

At or about 3:30 to 4:00 a.m., Lucky stumbles into the home he, his wife, and daughter shared. His composure was a wreck, his clothes wrinkled, wet, stained and he reeked of tequila, marijuana, and cigarette's. His wife yells, "Honey, is that you?" "It better be me?" he responded. "Not again! Please GOD, not again," she says. "ARE YOU DRUNK?!" She calmly asks him. "Shhh… Don't wake the baby," he says as he leans against the wall with one finger against his mouth. "Honey, why are you doing this to yourself. You've been clean for more than fifteen years." "I know babe. That is why I was celebrating," he says as he tries to walk by her but knocks a table over.

"Babe, look what you made me do," he says while lying on the floor. "I cannot accept this again. Are you doing this because of your friend?" He stares at her for a matter of seconds and begins to sob. "I let him down," he says incoherently. "That was not supposed to happen today. He was a good guy. What if he never wakes up?" He says, while banging his palm up against his forehead. Lucky tries to stand up but his wife holds him down. "LET ME GO. I'm going to see the judge right now and he's going to fix this babe...LET ME UP!"

"I will not. Are you trying to go to jail tonight, or better yet, get a bed next to your friend? Maybe y'all can both be laid up in a coma together? You smell like a wine-o for one, and for two, you're not going anywhere tonight but to sleep. So get your drunk self-up, pull yourself together and go get in bed," she demands. "But I gotta go talk to the judge babe, he's waiting on me," "No sir, you are NOT leaving this house, now do as I say and go to bed. If you go to the judge's home at this disrespectful time in the morning, in the condition you're in, he's going to have the entire police force come rough you up and take you far away from us. Is that what you want?" "No babe, they won't be able to handle me. I am going over there first thing in the morning though and he's going to have to deal with me, whether he likes it or not," he says as he gets up and stumbles towards the staircase. "It is first thing in the morning and you're not going over there. That man can ruin the rest of your life Lucky. You're not thinking clearly," she says as she helps him up the stairs. "I don't care, I'm going to give him a piece of my mind." "No, you're not honey, just go to bed and sleep this foolishness off." "I will, but when I get up I'm going to his house." "No, you're not. You're going to continue on with your life and let GOD deal with him... him and his unjust dealings."

CHAPTER 9

The next afternoon, Lucky awakes from his sleep. He's in so much pain, it hurts to open his eyes. It feels like someone has given him an acupuncture in his eyeballs. The pain is terrible. He screams for his wife Leslie, he gets no answer. He peeks out of his blinds, only to find her car is not in the driveway. He gets out of bed and reaches on the dresser for some medicine and finds a bottle of aspirin. He swallows a handful without even counting them. After taking them, he dives back into bed and throws the cover over his head, but not before pulling the waste basket next to him just in case. He tosses and turns but every movement makes him nauseous. He can't help it, he was restless. He felt his conscious eating at him from the inside out.

After about an hour of just lying there with his eyes wide shut, he finally musters up enough energy to drag himself to the edge of the bed. He vomits what feels like a couple of gallons of his insides into the trashcan. Afterwards, he sits back up, feeling better and worse at the same time. He looks out of the window, his wife is still gone. He walks over to the closet and finds a black t-shirt and black slacks, throws them on the bed, then goes and gets in the shower.

CHAPTER 10

As Leslie returned, she called Lucky on his phone as usual to come get the baby out of the car. She called him twice, but he didn't answer, he never did that before. Since they've been married she can count on one hand how many times that has happened. He always answered or called her back immediately, even when they were fighting. Something was wrong, and she knew it. "Oh no. Please GOD no," she prayed as she began to think.

Lucky sat in the lobby of the courtroom. Looking a mess and far out of character and place. He wore black from head to toe with a matching black fedora. He sat there patiently trying his best to look like he fit in. Maybe it was working because the lobby was full of people, but no one was staring, except for a few kids maybe, nothing out of the ordinary, yet.

Leslie sped down the freeway, trying her best to get to Lucky. She knew he would be in either one or two places, but she was more certain about one than the other. It was now one o'clock and she knew the court was in session.

She pulled into the parking garage hastily, barely using her breaks. She grabs the baby out of the car seat as quickly and safely as possible then darts towards the elevators. Upon arriving inside of the lobby of Judge Lamar's courtroom, she immediately looks around for him, there were so many people just standing around. Everything inside of her wanted to scream his name at the top of her lungs, but she knew that wouldn't be smart. She didn't want to cause a scene and if she did it would definitely scare the baby. None of those things would benefit her situation.

She calms herself, remembered how to breath and pulled herself together really quick for the sake of the situation. She slowly walked through the crowd, searching and searching. She didn't know what he was wearing so that was a slight problem. She had an idea, she could try to call him again. She takes out her I phone and calls him but this time it goes straight to voicemail. The worry begins to sit in again when suddenly she sees a man sitting on a bench, by himself in a corner. She makes a beeline straight towards him. He has on a black fedora exactly like the one Lucky own's, a black blazer, and black khakis. His head is down reading a magazine, so she can't see his face, but she is certain it's him from his square shoulders.

As she quickly approaches, the feelings of surety get stronger. "Lucky," she says as low as she possibly could. He just stared up at her with no expression. "Hey honey," she says as she sits in the empty seat next to him and grabs his hand. "What are you doing? Why haven't you answered my calls?" She asked simultaneously. "Why'd you bring the baby," he asked in a very low voice while staring at the double doors leading into the courtroom. "Because she wanted to see her daddy," she says as she placed her in his lap. He looks at Leslie, then looks at the baby in a trance like state. He then slowly places his hands around the baby's small waist, similar to the very first time he held her. When he reached to get her, Leslie saw the butt of the gun Lucky was hiding on the inside pocket of his blazer. She calmly placed her left hand on his chest, leaned in to kiss him, and removed the gun from his person, without him or anyone else noticing and tucked it inside of her purse. She takes a very deep breath, now with her hand over her own chest. She looks him into his eyes and says, "Come on honey, why don't you, me, and our precious daughter all go back home where we belong."

CHAPTER 11

The following weekend was Labor Day Weekend and Leslie and Lucky were having guest at their home. That week Lucky didn't come out of the room much and didn't have communication with no one besides a few of his employees. So, Leslie was happy to see him up and moving around. Before everyone arrived, he went to the grocery store and picked up a few last-minute things they needed while Leslie stayed home preparing everything for Lucky to barbecue that evening. At about five thirty that evening everybody began arriving. Leslie had beer, soda's, juices, waters, a few wine coolers on ice and some reclining patio chairs with pillows under a huge gazebo. It was a real comfortable setting. All of the children where inside playing board games and the adults were out back, laughing, joking, listening to music, some drinking, and a few couples were playing horse shoes by the fence.

Everyone was having a great time. By seven forty-five or eight o'clock the food was done. Everyone fed their kids first, then fixed themselves a plate. Everyone there thanked Lucky and Leslie for their hospitality, then they began to eat. Some outside on the patio, the rest sat inside at the huge dining room table. Everyone was eating, the kids, the adults, and the dog was having a field day, eating leftover chicken and rib bones. The time was now three minutes until nine o'clock and Leslie tells Lucky to change the television channel to the local news station. After turning to the channel the news was on, they watched one commercial then the local news began.

"Hello, I'm Chelsea Oliver and tonight at nine, police investigators are trying to piece together how a man who was not supposed to be driving got behind the wheel again. This time killing a young college student instantly. The young man was here visiting family during school break. They believe alcohol was involved and a brutal twist to this story, the young college student that was killed was the son of a local judge, Judge Lamar in the 9th district. Judge Lamar was the same judge that showed the driver leniency less than a month ago, handing him a very light punishment."

"Some are saying if he would have given him a stiffer sentence, he would've been locked up and unable to commit such a horrendous crime. After the driver, who name has yet to be released, hit a man last month, also under the influence, leaving him in a coma. There are a lot of questions to be asked and answered here tonight," Leslie looks over at Lucky, Lucky still staring at the television with a smirk on his face. Everyone around them are just chattering away, unaware of what just took place. Leslie leans in and whispers to Lucky, "Understand, a young and innocent man lost his life, so this is no reason at all to boast or celebrate," she says as she squeezes his arm. "But the power of Karma is real!"

CHAPTER 12

The following day, which was a Monday, Lucky had mixed feelings towards the situation. On one hand, he felt terrible for accepting any kind of satisfaction from the situation, because the world lost a young, bright child with a very promising future ahead of him. On the other hand, Lucky wanted retribution for his friend's injustice, which he got in the sleek form of a presence that seems to balance our rights and wrongs. Oh well, either way, what's done is done. We all learn from our mistakes and experiences.

It was the day after Labor Day so Lucky wanted to drop by see his friend and check on his condition. He gets off of the elevator and walks down the long depressing hallway he had to take to get to Grateful's wing. He walks straight pass the receptionist desk, no one ever stopped there anyway. As he approached the door he began to listen for the loud double beeps. He became nervous because he didn't hear them. He makes a two-step jolt into the room. He doesn't see him. He doesn't even see the bed. He jolts out of the room as fast as he jolted in and found the nearest nurses aid. "Ma'am, what happened to the patient that was in room #3379? He was in there less than a week ago and everything was fine. Where is he?"

"He's fine sir. He's up in recovery. I think Dr. Moulan is over that floor tonight," says the 5-foot 4 inch nurse's aide, as she taps the encased iPad she was holding with her manicured nails. "Just go straight ahead to the first set of elevators. Go to the seventh floor and ask any one at the receptionist desks and have them page

Dr. Moulan. He can help you." "Thank you darling," he says as he darts down the hallway to the elevators.

As he gets off of the elevator, a feeling of calmness over-takes him. He walks over to the picket fence white colored reception area where two young ladies are standing, laughing and talking. "Excuse me young ladies. By chance, could one of you be kind enough to page a Doctor Moulan please?" Lucky asks very dapperly. "Why sure," says the taller young lady in a very country accent. "Dr. Moulan to the west reception desk, please," she says over the loud speaker.

Approximately two and a half minutes later, a middle-aged clean faced gentleman wearing a Dallas Cowboys football cap comes around the corner walks over to the girl with the southern accent and Lucky sees her point over to him. "Hello sir, how may I help you this afternoon?" Dr. Moulan asks while extending his hand. "I'm doing good, thanks for asking. Do you have a patient by the name of Grateful Madden?" "Yes sir, I do. If you'll walk this way, you will find him hard at work. He has to learn his lower motor skills again, but he's coming along pretty good. After all, his first diagnosis re-vealed he would be paralyzed from the neck down or brain dead. So this is a pretty substantial blessing," says the Doctor. "That's very true Doctor. Any progression or progress is a blessing," says Lucky. "I think he's been waiting on you," says the Doctor before leading him into the room where Grateful was doing knee flexing exercises.

"Hey Friend," says Lucky as he burst into the room. "Look what the cat drug in," says Grateful as they give each other a hug. "I'll give you two a moment," says the nurse assisting Grateful. "I didn't even know you were awake. Why didn't you call me?" Asks Lucky. "They wouldn't give me my phone, plus I knew you would be here sooner or later," says Grateful as the nurse returns with a bottle of water and an ice cream cup. "Would you like anything sir?" The nurses aid asks Lucky. "Naugh, I'm fine thanks," responds Lucky.

The young lady placed the tray on the roller cart, sat it in front of Grateful and walks out of the room. Lucky asks Grateful "How are you feeling?" "Drugged up," Grateful responds. "I bet. You were out for a pretty good while brother. So it's going to take some time to get you back to one hundred percent. The best doctors are here for you," Lucky tells Grateful. "That's good to know and greatly appreciated. What I wanna know is, what happened to me," "You were hit by a drunk driver, which hit and killed another young man this past weekend," he explains. "You gotta be joking. Are you serious?" Asks Grateful. "I wouldn't lie to you my friend," says Lucky. "Where is he, did they catch him?" "We'll talk about it more later, I will fill you in on everything after you get more rest. Just know that none of man's bad deed's go unpunished, lucky for you my friend, all of man's good deeds will not go unrewarded."

CHAPTER 13

The following evening, Leslie and Lucky sat at the dinner table laughing and joking as if they were kids again on their first date. They prayed together, held hands, fed each other, and did all the things love birds do. They kissed and reminisced about the past, talked about the future. Everything was going well until Leslie mentioned the Judges wife, Sharon. She told him their youngest daughter needed a liver transplant very badly and that she had been on the waiting list for some time now. She also told him, she wanted to go with her (Sharon) on a blood drive. This is her way of showing support of what her family recently went through, losing their son. Lucky was against his wife having any dealings whatsoever with the judge or any one associated with him. After realizing there was no swaying her from her decision, Lucky abruptly ends their dinner, goes upstairs, and goes to bed.

The following evening, Lucky and Grateful sat in Grateful's hospital room chit-chatting and watching television, when the nurse comes in followed by Mr. Alexander. "Look who arose from the dead," says Mr. Alexander as he comes in and shakes Grateful's hand. "I would have given you a great big hug, but I don't know your condition and don't wanna hurt ya," he says while laughing as he goes over and shakes Lucky's hand. "I received a phone call last night from a longtime friend of mine that has twenty-five plus years in the medical field. On that phone call, my trusted friend, tells me there is a patient sitting in recovery right now that was diagnosed as being brain dead, at one time and progressed to being paralyzed from neck down, to today is in full recovery. He told me in his twenty-five years, he hasn't seen anything like it. As to human understanding, nothing about it is sensible," Mr. Alexander tells Grateful. "The Doctor told me the same thing. My recovery doesn't make sense, my recovery is considered a miracle. I want to say in my opinion, nothing about GOD IS sensible. He is in the impossible and miracle working business, that is what HE does daily. Not trying to gloat, but this is not a surprise to me, a real believer," responds Grateful. "We'll, if I wasn't a believer before, I am a believer now," says Mr. Alexander, with a huge grin on his face.

The three of them sat there talking for the next forty-five minutes before Mr. Alexander picks up his briefcase, opens it and neatly places some papers in front of Grateful. "I believe, right before one of us were briefly sidelined, we were in the middle of completing this very important paperwork that would bring the two of y'all geniuses idea to life. The only thing missing is one of our signatures," says Mr. Alexander as he sat a pen on top of the paperwork placed in front of Grateful.

CHAPTER 14

As Lucky arrives home, he is greeted with a note from Leslie stating she was going to be out for a while with Sharon. She will be helping her prepare for her upcoming event. He crumbles the note and throws it in the kitchen waste basket.

About an hour and a half later, Leslie comes home. Lucky is just getting done cooking dinner and preparing the table when she walks into the kitchen. "Where's my baby?," he asks as soon as he notices Leslie doesn't have the car seat. "I know you don't agree with me having a relationship with the Judges wife, so I didn't take her with me. I took her to my sister's, she's off this week, so she's going to keep her overnight to give us a break." "That was nice," says Lucky as he puts his finishing touches on the food. "Why don't you get washed up while I fix you a plate," he continued. Leslie takes off her shoes and walks down the hall to the bathroom to wash up. She smile as she left to get ready for dinner.

By the time Leslie comes out, Lucky already has the table set. "How was your day," she asked Lucky. "It was great. Very pro- ductive. Mr. Alexander came to the hospital while I was there and brought the unfinished paperwork for the project. Grateful was final- ly able to sign it and construction will began shortly," says Lucky with a huge smile on his face. "In a few years, the homeless population will decrease and we will become a lot wealthier," says Lucky. "That's great Honey," says Leslie. "Well, my day was very productive also. Sharon and I got everything prepared. We hung decorations and

made snacks for most of the afternoon and in the early part of the evening we set up the testing booths. The lady is doing all of this out of her own pocket," she tells Lucky. "And we were blessed to have the guys that delivered the testing products volunteer and test themselves as a show of support to Sharon and her daughter."
"Sweetheart, I love you like no other woman ever created. You follow me," he asks. "Yes, I know you do honey," "And we both know I don't agree with who you've allied yourself with lately, but I do respect what you two are doing. I would rather not talk about them before I eat my dinner. I apologize if you don't like it, but it's the truth."

"I just don't get what you have against this sweet lady. She's out here fighting for her daughter's life, on the heels of losing a son. That precious little baby has less than six months to live if she doesn't get a new liver. She has nothing to do with her husband's dealings. She has her life and he has his. Look at it this way they just happen to be married to one another. You're acting like a silly little teenage girl," says Leslie as she grabs a scoop of potatoes. "She only has six months?" Asks Lucky. "Yes. If she doesn't get a better liver, they will have lost both of their children in the same year," says Leslie with tears in her eyes. "Wow, I didn't realize it was that deep," says Lucky. "You didn't try to realize it. You simply had a problem with her because of what her husband did." Lucky looks his wife in the eyes. "You are absolutely right sweetheart. May GOD have mercy on that woman and her family."

CHAPTER 15

After exactly ninety days of physical and mental rehabilitation, Lucky is released from the hospital with a full recovery. Grateful picks him up from the hospital. "My wife's frying some fish and cooking seafood, wanna stop by and grab a bite before I take you home?" Asks Lucky. "Might as well., I could use a home cooked meal. That hospital food was terrible," says Grateful as they laugh and enjoy the ride to Lucky's.

As they enter Lucky's home it's dark and quiet. "Did you forget to pay the light bill?" asked Grateful. "Not at all," says Lucky before hitting the lights. "SURPRISE!!!," screams a room full of people. "OH MY," yells Grateful as he jumps backwards. "I just wanted to show you we care," says Lucky as he gives Grateful a great big hug. "Thank you friend," says Grateful.

After a few hours of dancing and partying, Grateful goes to the back patio to get some air. Leslie and Lucky where already out there. "There y'all go. I would say I've been looking for y'all, but I haven't. Hahaha," Grateful laughs. "I'm just kidding guys. Am I interrupting you two?" Asks Grateful. "Naugh buddy. Not at all. We were just taking in some of fresh air, but while you're out here, I wanna get your opinion on something." "Go ahead I'm listening," responds Grateful. "If you feel like someone has wronged you or someone close to you and later down the road, you notice that person needed help in a major way, would you help them?" "That's a decision a person has to put on their big boy draws to make. One thing this person has to realize and keep in mind is, we are here to help one another. It doesn't matter if they've wronged you or not, you must help in any way possible. To fully serve your purpose, you must be a functioning servant to your GOD, your brothers and sisters. So that person can be an unhumble knucklehead and ignore the calls of his or her brother or sister's distress, or do what GOD love's and be kind," explains Grateful. "You have an answer for everything don't you?," says Lucky.

CHAPTER 16

That night, Lucky lay in bed and Grateful's words were re-
playing in his head, repeatedly. He couldn't forget the horrible look
of disappointment on Leslie's face when all of her and Sharon's hard
work went unsuccessful. He was restless, he felt like he needed to do
something. He felt like he needed to help.

The very next morning, after a sleepless night, as soon as his
alarm went off, he was out the bed and getting dressed. "What's the
hurry?" Asks Leslie. "Something very, very, very important has come
up," says Lucky. "More important than eating breakfast... or loving
your wife," asks Leslie before removing the silk sheets that where
concealing her nude body. "You know what baby?" asks Lucky while
stopping to adore the lovely view. "What?" "There's nothing anyone
can say or do to make me disbelieve that I have the sexiest and most
gorgeous wife on earth, nothing. Seriously, right now I gotta act on
this sense of urgency while it's on my mind," says Lucky. He throws
on his hat and bolts out of the room. Leslie lay there as confused as
she'd ever been. She trusted her husband and if he said it was important, then it must be important. Not even thirty seconds after
bolting from the room, he bolts back in and dives onto his wife, ful-
filling his "husbandly" duties.

Later that morning, about nine forty-five, Lucky picks up
Grateful and calls Mr. Alexander and asked him to meet them at the
construction site where they are constructing the huge homeless facility. "I brought y'all out this morning to talk about a matter I consider

to be very serious. There is a young lady that desperately needs our help. She is battling a very rare disease and it's causing her kidneys to work so hard that one of them gave out. If she doesn't get another one very soon, her precious little life may come to an end," says Lucky as he continues to tell them everything he knows about the situation.

"Well, I'm aboard," says Mr. Alexander. The both of them look at Grateful. "Of course, I'm with it," says Grateful. "Ok, let's get this show on the road," says Lucky. The three of them load into Lucky's truck and head towards their destination.

CHAPTER 17

Later that afternoon, Lucky and Mr. Alexander arranged for a section of the construction site to be transformed into a make shift testing center. They asked all the workers if they would agree to help with their cause. They have close to one thousand people agreeing to be tested. All of this in the name of helping a little girl whose name he did not even know.

Before they got started, Lucky called Leslie to see if she and Sharon would be interested in coming down and joining them. Of course, he got a resounding yes from his wife.

As the two women arrive at the construction site they are overwhelmed by the support of all these complete strangers. Leslie finds Lucky and runs up to him and gives him the biggest and tightest hug she's ever given before. Sharon with tears flowing down her cheek does the same. "GOD bless you sir," says Sharon, unable to hold back the tears.

About an hour into the testing, Lucky sees a familiar face approaching, it's Judge Lamar. Once they made eye contact, it was never broken until they were face to face.

"What you are doing sir speaks volumes to my family and this community. You don't have to do this," says the Judge. "You're absolutely right," says Lucky. "But what kind of man would stand around and do nothing while he could be helping. After all, that little girl did nothing to me. The actions of her father should not penalize her," says Lucky as the Judge finally breaks eye contact and looks to the sky. "You know, life can be really tricky and deceiving at times. The guy that killed my son is the grandson of a very influential and powerful man. A man that guaranteed me a top seat in the mayor's office. He asked for one thing from me. He wanted to make sure his one and only grandson didn't go to prison. Sure, I could've brushed him off and went by the book, but I didn't. I chose success over humanity and it cost me my dear son's life."

"Do you know how many times I've prayed since my son's death?" Asks the Judge. "I would hope plenty," answers Lucky. "Well your wrong. I have not prayed one single time. I feel embarrassed going to GOD after my actions. I knew what I was doing was wrong. I knew that that man would get out and drink and drive again. I never thought one decision would affect me so viciously," says the Judge. He then lowers his head and kicks at a rock protruding from the reddish-brown dirt. "You outdid yourself this time Lucky," says Grateful as he walks up. "Grateful, I have someone here I think you should meet," says Lucky. "Okay," says Grateful as he looks at Judge Lamar. "This is the Honorable Judge Lamar. Judge Lamar, meet the man behind all the madness, Grateful." They look at each other without saying a word at first, not even a facial expression.

Then Grateful breaks the short silence. "My condolences to you regarding your son," as he extends his hand. "Thank you kindly," says the Judge. "My apologies to you. You deserved a lot more justice than I gave you." "No apology needed. Unfortunately, you caught the rawest end of the deal. I don't need an apology," says Grateful. "Thank you for not jumping on my back. You easily could have," says the Judge. "That would've fixed nothing, plus why ruin a perfectly planned day of testing," says Grateful with a smile on his face. "Valid point," says Lucky as the three of them walk off, giving Judge Lamar a tour of the freshly renovated testing site.

CHAPTER 18

Approximately two days later, the results came back. They found a donor who matches every requirement for a perfect fit. It was a success, little Sara will live, and in a few months, she should be one hundred percent healthy. To celebrate, the Judge and his wife invite Lucky, Grateful, Mr. Alexander, and their families over for a nice dinner.

After everyone finished eating, the Judge stands and makes an announcement. "Can I have everyone's attention please? Today is a great day for my family. It's been a rough month, but I believe everything happens for a greater purpose. I truly thank GOD for my wife, HE gave me the best and strongest backbone a man could ask for," the Judge says while looking into his wife's eyes. Then he turns to Lucky, Grateful, and Mr. Alexander and takes off his glasses. "You three gentlemen... words cannot express how thankful I am for you all. You gave me and my beautiful wife a reason to continue living. For a while I was watching my life completely shatter and fall apart and there was nothing I could do about it. We lost our prince and was on the verge of losing our princess. I don't think I could've bounced back from that."

"I told my wife I felt like I was a major contributor to my son's death. She kept telling me I wasn't, but we both knew I was. If I would've just did my job properly, my son would still be here today." The Judge continues speaking with tears in his eyes. "So, I must say. Thank you, guys, very much. You always will be special to this family." Immediately after sitting down his wife stands and says, "I can't let this opportunity pass without saying something to you gentleman and my new friend Leslie." "When I got the call a little after midnight a few weeks ago, I was crushed. The feeling of your heart leaving your body is a feeling of pure desperation. You can't breathe, your vision is out of whack... you can't even hear. I still haven't been able to eat a full meal since he left us. It's very painful."

"On top of that, the thought of losing another child took every sensation of living away from me. We exhausted every route available and then some. We faced disappointment, frustration, anger, confusion, etc... every emotion you can think of has trickled through my bones. Then you guys come along. Leslie, you're such a sweetheart. From the moment I told you my situation, you were there for me. I have an undying love for you beyond forever for that. Everything about you has been genuine," said Sharon. Then she turned her attention to Grateful and Lucky. "Please don't hold any type of grudge against my husband. I understand you may feel justice was not served in your case, but my husband truly is a good man. He only did what he did for the betterment of this family. It was nothing personal. I pray you truly understand."

CHAPTER 19

Eighteen months later...

Grateful, his new fiancé Bianca, Lucky, Leslie and Mr. Alexander met at the construction site to view the finished product. It's a success. It is a three thousand square foot building sitting on a five thousand square foot lot. Everything has finally come together.

"Two years ago, this was merely a vision, today it's a reality," says Lucky as he and Grateful stand in front of the building preparing to cut the ribbons. They were officially opening the center for business. The project manager approaches the two with scissors in hand and announces, "Today is a day of great change. This building is the first of its kind. This will be the beginning of a new life for many people thanks to the effort of these gentleman." He smiles and hands over the scissors. Lucky takes them and says to Grateful, "This was all your idea buddy, so I think it would be only right if you did the honors and cut the ribbon." He nods and hands Grateful the scissors. "It would be my pleasure," says Grateful as he takes the scissors from Lucky. They both paused taking a deep breath before Grateful cut the ribbon. "The Grateful House is officially open," says the project manager as they receive applause from the small crowd who came to in show their support.

After officially opening their doors for business, they offer free lunch to anyone that shows up at their doors. They also offer to those who need clothes, shoes, jackets, blankets and food vouchers.

"You know, I don't think this day could get any better," says Lucky. "You're right, it's going to be hard to top this feeling," says Grateful as he continues to look with amazement at the finished building. "Indeed," says Lucky as the project manager approaches them. "Everything with the construction went picture perfect as planned, except for one minor problem," he says to the two of them. "What's that?," asks Lucky with a look of concern on his face. "Well, it's nothing to worry yourselves about right now, but if not taken care of in the near future it can possibly be a problem." "Talk to us bro, let us know what's up," says Lucky. "Well, a few tests came back and some of our readings revealed there is pressure building up in some of the underground pipes. Now, it's nothing to stress over in the near future, but you guys may have some problems with your foundation if it's not fixed soon," says the project manager. Lucky looks at him and smiles and says, "No worries, I have the perfect guy for the job!!!"

About The Author

About me…

    I am a 37-year-old father, son, poetician, and writer. I am from a small town in southeast Arkansas. Moved to North Texas at an early age and continued my journey in life. I love the art of writing. With it, an artist can be creative in so many ways. I have been writing since 2013 and have become addicted. If you love great stories stay tuned, there's so much more to come.

    I was blessed with nine kids, eight girls and one boy. The oldest is eighteen and youngest are 6, twin boy and girl. I am the eldest sibling of five sisters and four brothers. My objective is to motivate the next generation to be Great. Any and all things are possible with the right amount of effort and drive. If you believe it you can achieve it. There's nothing more powerful than a focused mind!

Contact Information:

Email: *youngdameon81@gmail.com*

Facebook: *www.facebook.com/dameonyoung*

Instagram: **www.instagram.com/dameonyoung**

Twitter: **www.twitter.com/** *dameony*

YouTube: **www.youtube.com/** *Poetic Mindstate*